You Belong

Judy Young
2021

D1362033

To Scott, Mark, Laura, and Matt, for the joy of belonging with you.

You Belong

by Judy Young

Illustrated by Sally Becker

You belong in my lap
in the old rocking chair
that sits in the room
at the top of the stair.

Downstairs where we eat
are your highchair and mouse.
Dad reads on the couch,
you belong in this house.

Squirrels squabble outside,
jumping over your swing.
You belong in this yard
with birds on the wing.

Weaving branches with ours,
trees lean over the gate.
You belong in the schoolyard next door
where you ride trikes with Kate.

Kids come here on buses,
at the corner you wave.
You belong with Ann, the bus driver,
and garbage man Dave.

Up the hill Ride-on buses
pick up Dad and his friends,
they'll ride to the train
when a new day begins.

You belong in this neighborhood,

right by the town

where Dad's train lets him out,

and he's back above ground.

He hears bikes and traffic.
Construction men pound.
You belong on the train,
how you love all that sound!

And you belong in Dad's building.

People rushing about

all stop to say hi.

"It's Juan's son!" goes the shout.

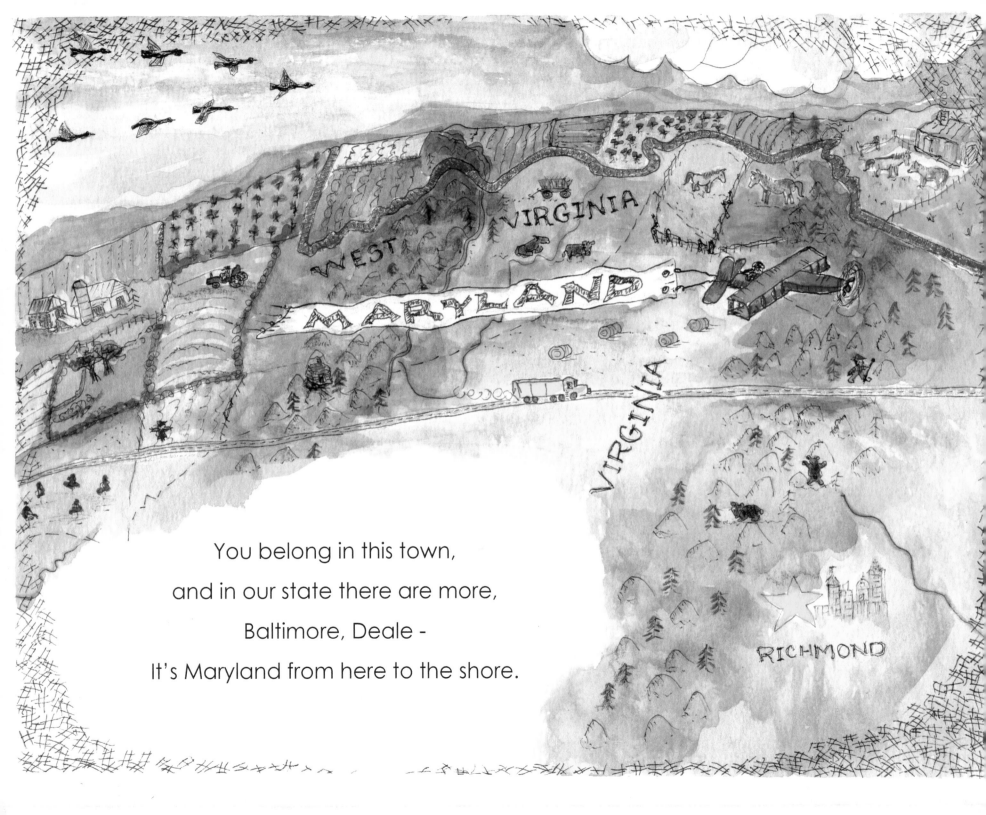

You belong in this town,
and in our state there are more,
Baltimore, Deale -
It's Maryland from here to the shore.

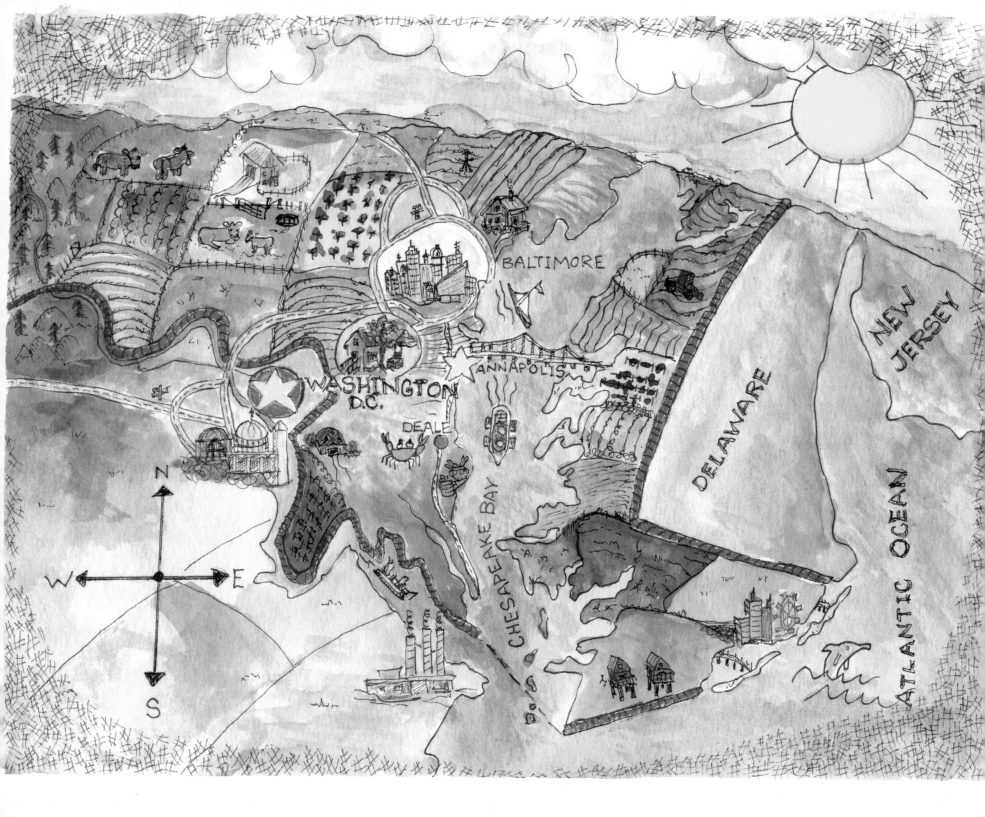

There across the Bay Bridge
Grandma lives, near the beach.
You belong with the shells,
finding patterns in each.

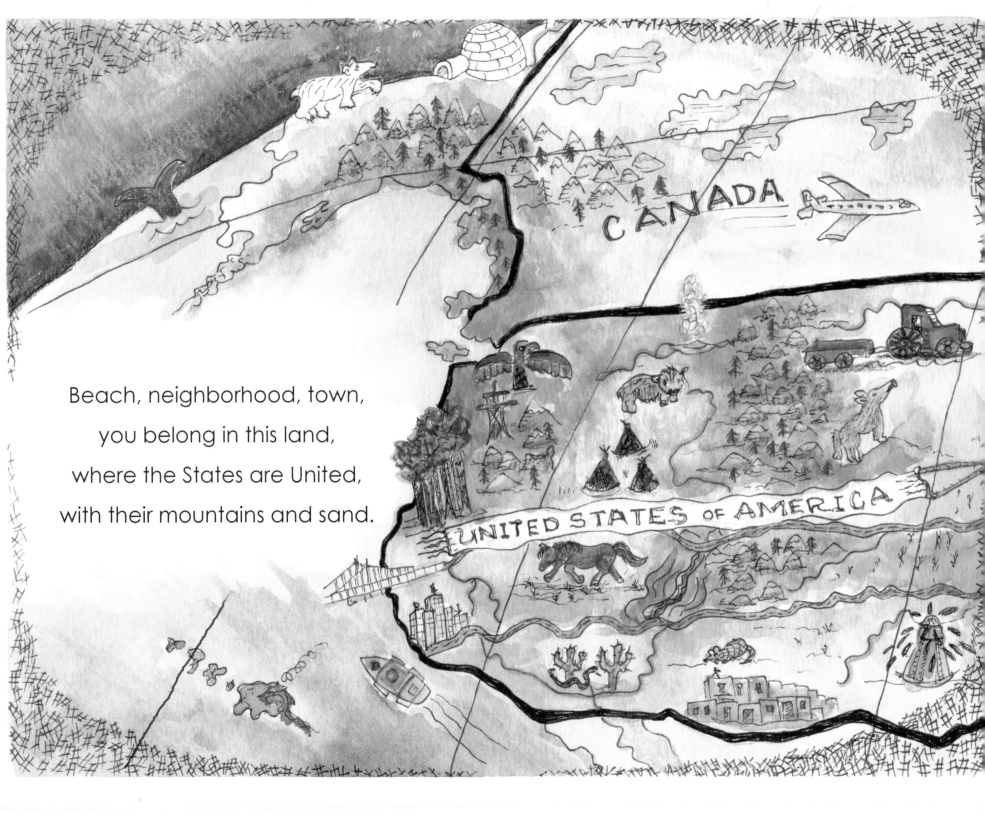

Beach, neighborhood, town,
you belong in this land,
where the States are United,
with their mountains and sand.

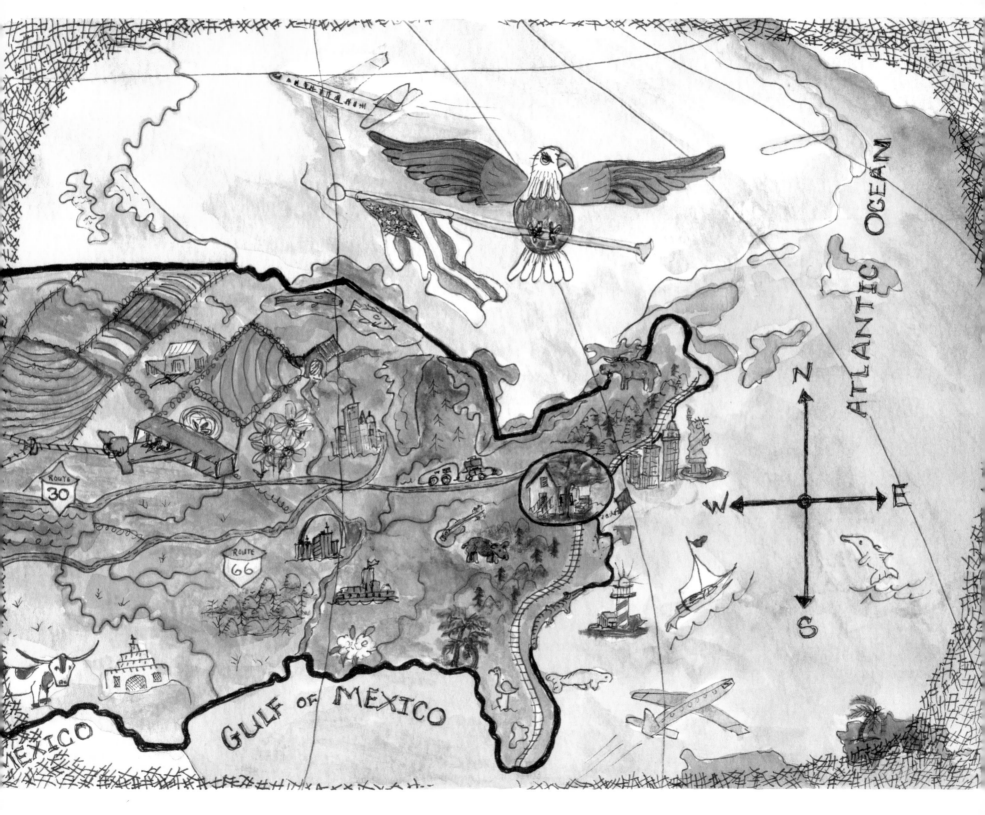

Across the big ocean
other lands belong too,
other mothers and fathers,
other children like you.

All belong in this world,
these lands washed by the sea,
one of eight planets,
the Sun's merry bee.

And other stars glimmer up in the night sky
telescopes see them.
So do you,
So do I.

You belong with these stars,

on this Earth, by our Sun.

You belong in the states -

and in this very one.

You belong on our street
in your room, in this house,
with Dad reading downstairs
by your highchair and mouse.

And you belong in my lap
in the old rocking chair
that sits in the room
at the top of the stair.

Judy and her husband David currently live across the border from Maryland in Gettysburg, PA. Their two sons grew up in Silver Spring, Maryland. There, like the father in *You Belong*, David would take the Ride-On bus and the Metro to work in downtown Washington D.C. daily. The family also served in the Foreign Agricultural Service for four years in Costa Rica and three years in New Zealand. Judy's mother lived across the Bay Bridge on the Eastern Shore of Maryland.

Sally Becker is an artist and art educator who grew up on a farm in South Central Pennsylvania. She creates art using a variety of media and uses her surroundings and memories of farm life as the subjects for her art. She enjoys exhibiting her work in nearby galleries and shows. Judy Young's words in *You Belong* inspired Sally to use images from her own family's life in her illustrations. The recurring red wooden child's swing is one example.

With thanks to Scott Young and Linnea Carlson for their kind technical assistance.

CPSIA information can be obtained
at www.ICGtesting.com
Printed in the USA
BVRC090857211021
619473BV00001B/1